The VAMPIRE'S LAIR

by Dee Phillips

illustrated by Timo Grubing

BEARPORT
PUBLISHING

New York, New York

Credits
Cover, © leoks/Shutterstock, © Benny Thaibert/Shutterstock, and © biosdi/Shutterstock.

Publisher: Kenn Goin
Editor: Jessica Rudolph
Creative Director: Spencer Brinker

Library of Congress Cataloging-in-Publication Data in process at time of publication (2017)
Library of Congress Control Number: 2016020325
ISBN-13: 978-1-944102302

For more information, write to Bearport Publishing Company, Inc., 45 West 21st Street, Suite 3B, New York, New York 10010.
Printed in the United States of America.

10 9 8 7 6 5 4 3 2 1

Contents

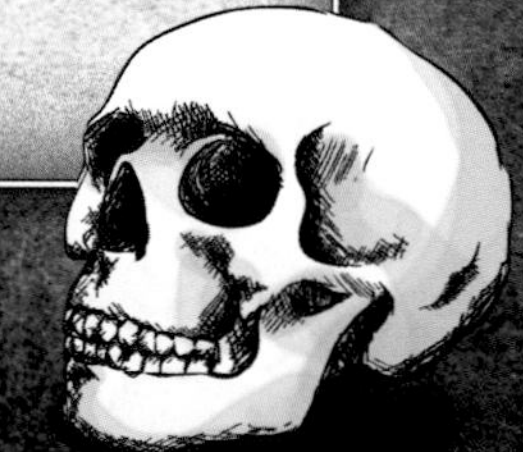

Jack pressed his face to the car window. Mile after mile of dark forest flashed by. He checked the clock on the dashboard. Two hours had passed since they'd left the airport, and now the sun was going down.

"How much longer, Dad?" Jack asked.

Dad caught Jack's eye in the rearview mirror. "About thirty minutes," he said.

Jack was excited. Soon they would be at Castle Prahova. He gave his twin brother, Dylan, a nudge with his elbow. Dylan, who was dozing after their long journey from the United States, slowly opened his eyes.

"I can't believe your sister is getting married in Romania—in a castle!" said the boys' mom.

In less than twenty-four hours, the twins' older sister, Penny, would marry her Romanian **fiancé**, Razva. The wedding was taking place in a mountaintop castle a few miles from the tiny village where Razva had grown up. Everyone was eager to see Penny and to meet Razva for the first time.

"Here," said Mom to the boys. She passed them a brochure. "This is all about the castle and its history."

Jack slowly turned the pages, which showed photos of weddings and other parties that had been held in the old castle. Then the heading on one of the pages jumped out at him:

The Vampire of Castle Prahova

"Listen to this," said Jack, reading from the brochure. "More than five hundred years ago, the castle was home to a Romanian prince. The prince had a beautiful daughter with long black hair and pale skin. The people of the village became **suspicious** of the young woman because she never left the castle except to walk in the forest at night."

"Then, one morning, a group of villagers made a **gruesome** discovery on the edge of the forest. They found the body of a young shepherd. Every drop of blood had been drained from the boy's **corpse**!"

"Eeww!" said Dylan.

"The villagers were convinced the prince's daughter was responsible for the shepherd's death," Jack continued reading. "They believed she was a vampire and wanted to kill her. To protect his daughter from the villagers, the prince locked her up in a secret room in the castle."

"Cool," said Dylan, enjoying the tale. "What happened in the end?"

"After the prince died, no one ever found his daughter. It is said that to this day, the vampire remains imprisoned somewhere in the castle."

"Hey guys," said Dad. "Look up ahead."

Jack and Dylan gasped. The road had gradually grown steeper and now the car was climbing toward a tall cliff. Perched on top, as if it had grown out of the rock, was Castle Prahova.

Dad drove through the castle gates and stopped the car in a small **courtyard**.

"Mom! Dad!" Penny came running across the courtyard. "It's so great to see you all!" she said as she kissed and hugged her parents and brothers.

In the shadows beneath the castle's steep walls, Jack noticed a dark figure watching his family. Penny followed Jack's gaze.

"Everyone," she said, motioning to the figure, "this is Razva."

Razva stepped out of the shadows. He was tall and thin. His long black hair grew down to his shoulders, and his pale skin had an almost blueish-gray tone.

The twins watched as Razva shook hands with their father. Then, he took hold of their mother's hand and bent to kiss it. "I am honored to meet Penny's family," he said with a thick accent.

Penny excitedly led her mother off toward the castle, while her father began unloading bags from the trunk.

Razva studied the boys. Jack felt as if the man's black eyes were burning into him. "So, you are Penny's brothers," he said slowly.

The boys nodded nervously. They were usually confident, but now the twins could think of nothing to say.

Razva stared past the courtyard entrance toward the distant, misty forest.

"Welcome to Transylvania," he said.

CHAPTER 2

Razva

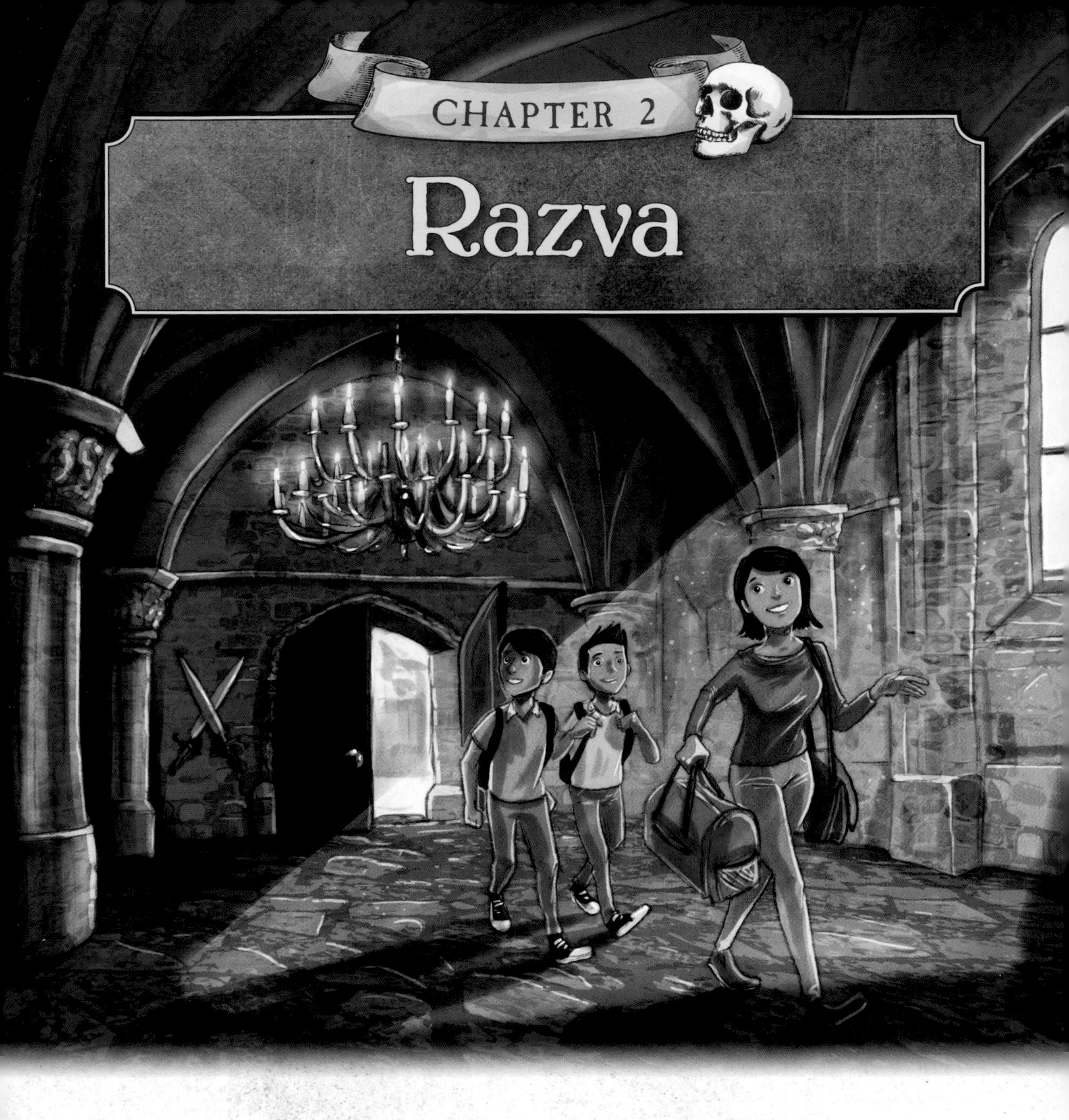

Jack and Dylan stepped into the front hallway of the castle. The flickering light from dozens of candles in a large chandelier danced across the high ceiling. Swords, axes, and other **medieval** weapons hung from the rough stone walls.

"Come on, you two," said Penny, helping the boys with their bags. "We're all sleeping upstairs."

Jack and Dylan followed Penny through a heavy wooden door into a gloomy tower.

"It's quite a climb," Penny said as she walked up the narrow stairway that spiraled around and around. At the top of the stairs, they stepped into a long, shadowy corridor.

"Here's your room," said Penny, pointing to a door on the left. "Mom and Dad are staying right next door."

Penny dashed back to the top of the stairway. "Be downstairs for dinner in twenty minutes," she said.

Jack pushed open the bedroom door. In the center of the room were two large canopy beds. Dusty **tapestries** showing medieval battle scenes hung on the walls.

Jack rushed to one of the beds. "This is mine!" he shouted.

"What's that?" asked Dylan, pointing to a small wooden box on a table.

Jack opened the lid and peered inside.

The box contained a cross, some small glass bottles, and several pieces of wood with sharp points at one end.

Jack removed the cork stopper from one of the bottles and sniffed. "Yuck!" he said, offering Dylan a sniff of the bottle's contents.

"What's that smell?" asked Dylan.

"It is garlic," said a voice behind them.

Jack and Dylan nearly jumped out of their skins. They quickly spun around to see Razva standing in the doorway.

"I see you have found one of the castle's vampire-killing kits," he said.

Jack placed the bottle of garlic powder back into the box. "A vampire-killing kit?" he said quietly.

Razva entered the room and stood next to the boys. "My country's history is filled with stories of vampires," he said. "Travelers in these mountains used to carry the kits to ward off and kill the evil creatures."

"What's the garlic for?" asked Dylan.

Razva stared hard into Dylan's eyes. "Garlic can be used to keep a bloodsucker at bay," he answered.

"And the cross?" gulped Jack.

"A cross is a powerful sign of goodness," answered Razva.

"A vampire will not come close to a cross."

Dylan reached out to touch one of the sharp wooden spikes. "This is a wooden **stake** for killing a vampire isn't it?" he said to Razva. "It has to be stabbed into a vampire's heart!"

Razva quickly shut the lid of the box with his long, bony fingers.

"Razva?" said Dylan. "We read that there's a five hundred-year-old vampire locked up somewhere in this castle. Do you think the story is true?"

For just the briefest moment, Razva's pale face showed alarm. Then he said, "That is nothing but an old **legend**."

He walked to the bedroom door and turned to look back at the twins.

"My apologies, boys," he said. "I should not be filling your heads with all this nonsense about vampires. Of course . . . none of it is true!"

Then he gave them a weak smile and hurried out of the room.

It was nearing dawn, and Jack and Dylan were huddled under their blankets. Neither had been able to sleep that night. They were both too occupied thinking about the events earlier that evening.

The dinner in the castle's main hall had gone well. As the evening drew on, more and more guests had arrived for the wedding. Despite all the excitement, however, the boys had found themselves watching Razva at every opportunity. All night, their sister's fiancé had seemed uneasy. He'd disappeared from the room for several minutes at a time. And he hadn't eaten a single bite of food.

Now, the castle was still and silent, but the boys couldn't relax.

"Did you lock the door?" Jack asked Dylan.

Dylan got out of his bed and crept to the heavy wooden door. He twisted the handle. Then, satisfied that the door was locked tight, he hurried back to the bed.

Eventually, Jack said, "Dylan, I don't like this place."

With relief, Dylan agreed. "Yeah, it seemed cool at first, but there's something creepy about Razva and . . . ."

Click. Click. The metal doorknob on the bedroom door turned one way and then another.

Jack and Dylan froze and looked at each other in terror. Someone—or something—was trying to open their door!

Click. Click. The doorknob turned again.

Afraid to make a sound, the boys listened. The clicking stopped, and they heard footsteps move away from the door.

Jack was shaking, but he wanted to find out what was going on. "Come on," he said to Dylan. "Maybe that was Mom or Dad. Let's go see."

The boys crept across the room. Jack carefully unlocked the door and pushed it open just a few inches. Then he stuck his head out into the corridor. To Jack's horror, he saw a dark figure try to open the door to their parents' room, then head for the stairwell in the tower. As the person passed a narrow window, bright moonlight lit up his face. It was Razva!

"Let's go," whispered Jack as he put on his shoes. He tried to sound much braver than he actually felt. "Razva was at the door. We have to find out what he's up to."

CHAPTER 3

The Prisoner

The boys followed Razva down the stairwell, trying hard to stay out of view and to not make a sound.

At the bottom of the stairs, Razva walked through the castle's front hallway and disappeared outside. Following a few seconds behind, the boys stepped outside into the courtyard. Razva was nowhere to be seen. It was as if he had simply melted into the night air.

As the twins searched the shadows, Jack was sure he saw a faint light coming from inside the stone well in the center of the courtyard. He peered down into the well's murky depths, but just then the light disappeared. Jack leaned over to get a closer look when a stone crumbled beneath his weight. He fell forward and tumbled down into the well.

"Ahhhh!" screamed Jack as he plunged into the darkness.

Thud! He landed at the bottom of the well in a

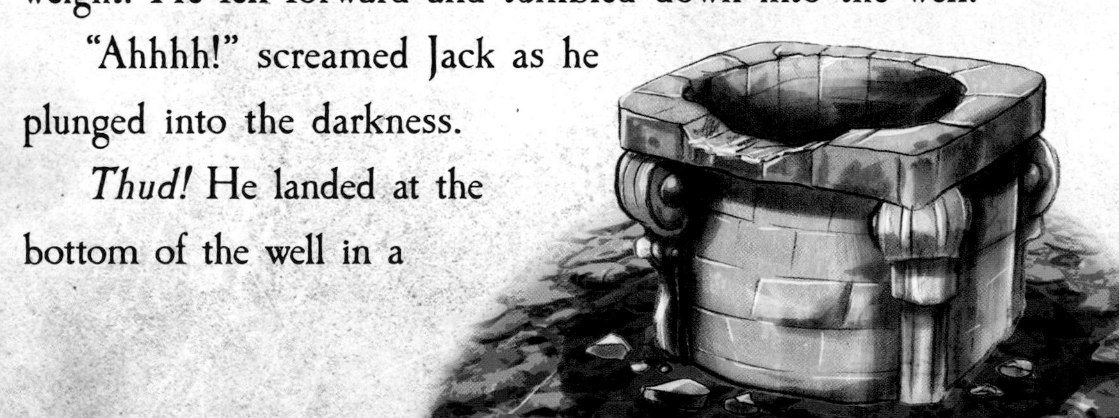

layer of mud. Within seconds, Dylan's worried face was peering down the well at him.

"Jack? Jack? Are you okay?" called Dylan.

"Yes, I think so," answered Jack, rubbing his elbow.

Jack pulled his cell phone from his pants and switched on the flashlight. He could see that a rusty metal ladder was attached to the slime-covered stone wall. As he shined the light around, Jack saw two narrow tunnels leading off from the bottom of the well.

"Dylan, get down here quick," said Jack. "There are tunnels!" He aimed the flashlight at the metal ladder so his brother could see it. "You can climb down."

Dylan carefully scrambled over the crumbling stonework and descended into the well.

Jack shined his flashlight into one of the tunnels. "Come on," he said to Dylan. "I saw a light before. Maybe Razva went into a tunnel."

The dark passageway was so narrow that the walls almost touched the boys' shoulders as they crept along.

After walking for a few minutes, they came upon a door at the end of the tunnel. It was locked tight by several large iron bolts.

"Let's go back," said Dylan, his voice shaking. "Razva probably isn't down here."

But Jack's hand was already reaching for the top bolt. "I want to know what's in here," he said quietly.

With a lot of effort, the boys slid each bolt aside and opened the door. A terrible smell of rotting meat filled their nostrils.

Behind the door was a tiny room. The stub of a flickering candle cast a dim light on the walls, and thick gray cobwebs hung from the ceiling. There was a canopy bed surrounded by flimsy drapes at the far wall. Jack crept toward the bed and gently pulled one of the drapes aside.

"Oh . . . oh . . . OH!" he cried, staggering backward with a look of fear on his face.

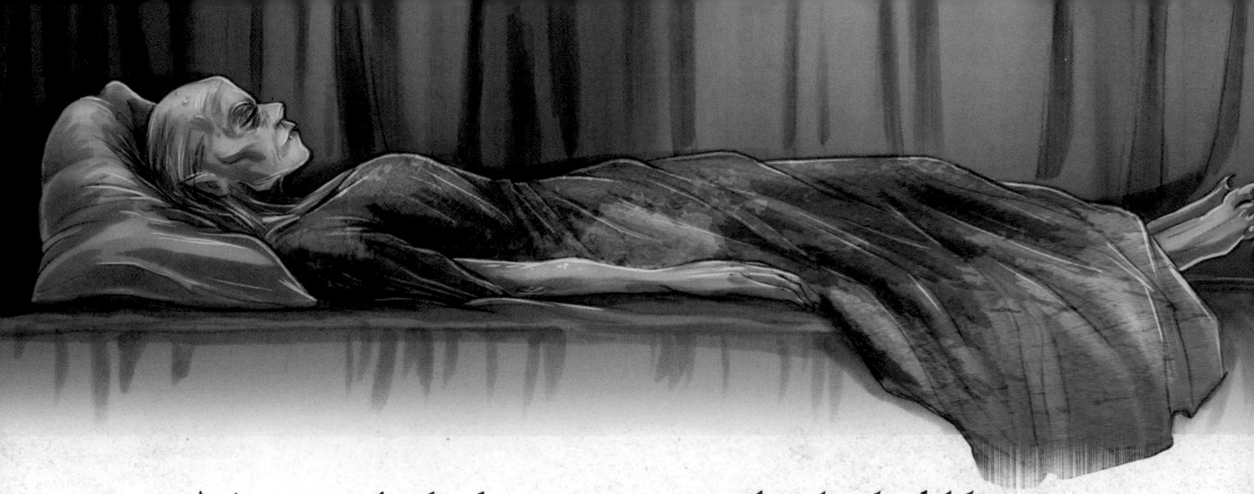

Asleep on the bed was a creature that looked like a woman wearing a long, ragged green dress. The arms and hands that stuck out from the sleeves were just bones wrapped in **ancient**, papery skin. A few strands of hair hung from her head.

"It's her!" whispered Jack. "It's the vampire!" He grabbed Dylan's arm. "We have to get out of here," he cried.

But before the boys could run, the vampire opened her mouth, revealing four long, perfect white fangs. Her head twisted toward the boys and her eyes flickered open.

"I smell you," she hissed. "Come to me."

Howling with terror, Jack and Dylan scrambled through the door and started running down the tunnel.

The rough, rocky walls of the narrow passageway tore at the boys' hands and clothes as they ran. The hissing voice and awful **stench** of the vampire was close behind them. Soon, they burst out of the narrow tunnel into the well and crashed straight into Razva, who was coming from the other direction.

"Run!" screamed Jack. "There's a vampire right behind us!"

"Come to me!" hissed the vampire, emerging from the tunnel.

Razva pulled a cross from his jacket and held it up in front of the monster.

She shrank backward and raised her skeletal hands to cover her face.

"We can get out this way," yelled Razva. He pushed the boys ahead of him into the other tunnel.

"Keep running," he shouted. "Don't look back!"

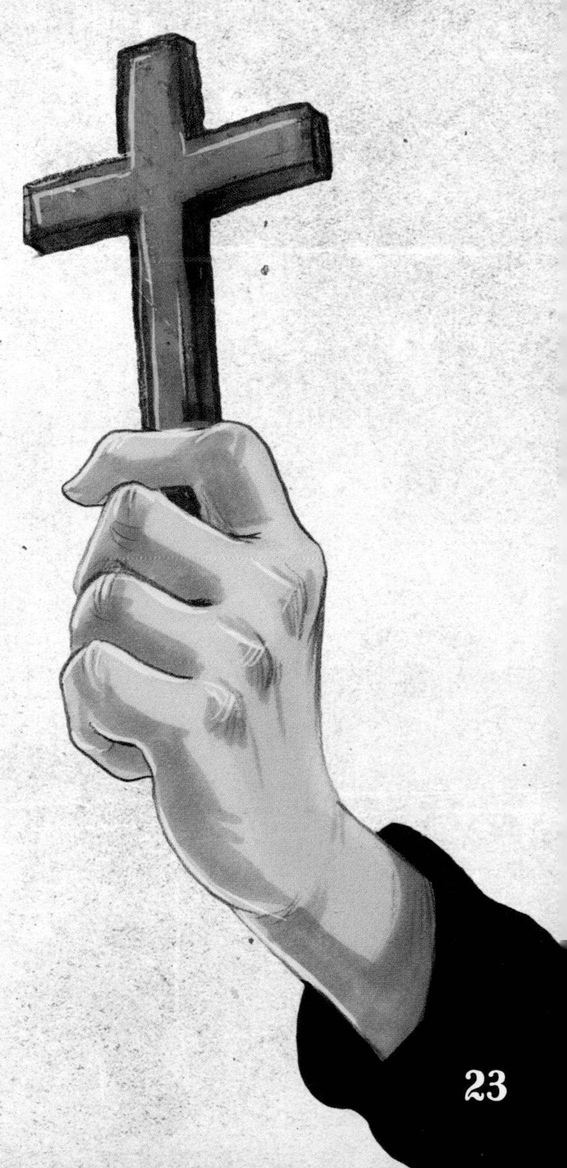

CHAPTER 4
Vampire Hunters

The tunnel twisted and turned until they reached another heavy wooden door. Razva ran ahead, heaved open the door, and pushed the boys through it.

Jack and Dylan gasped as they took in their surroundings. A skeleton dangled from one wall, its wrists and ankles shackled to the stonework by chains. A **rack** that was once used to tear apart the bodies of prisoners filled one corner. The boys stared in horrified awe at an enormous **iron maiden** in the center of the room. The iron maiden's doors hung open to reveal dozens of long, sharp metal spikes. The brothers realized they were in a torture chamber in the castle's **dungeon**!

Before the boys and Razva could catch their breath, the hideous creature burst into the dungeon.

"I must feed!" she wailed, hurling herself at Razva and wrapping her bony fingers around his neck.

Razva struggled to break free as the vampire lowered her fangs toward his neck.

"Tackle her!" screamed Jack. The brothers rushed at the

vampire and shoved her straight into the open iron maiden.

Razva was right behind them, and together they slammed the doors of the iron maiden tightly shut.

"Aaarrrrgghhhhhh!" A miserable howl erupted from the torture device as the metal spikes pierced the vampire's body.

"We've got her!" shouted Jack.

Razva shook his head. "That will not kill her," he warned. "We have to use a wooden stake or . . . "

Just then, Razva noticed a shaft of sunlight entering the dungeon through a slit of a window in the thick castle wall. The beam of light grew longer and stronger, creeping across the stone floor toward the iron maiden.

"That's it," said Razva. "If a vampire's skin is exposed to sunlight, the creature will burn!"

Razva directed the boys to each take hold of one of the iron maiden doors. "When I say "Now," open the doors," he said.

Within seconds, the iron maiden was bathed in sunshine. Razva stood before the device and shouted, "Now!"

The boys pulled the doors open and saw the vampire. **Puncture** holes from the metal spikes covered her entire body. But her terrifying strength had not diminished. She sprang toward Razva's throat—directly into the bright, early morning light.

Screeching, she tried to cover her face with her hands. The smell of burning flesh filled the air. Flames and sparks exploded from her body as her skin melted and her bones turned to ash.

In less than a minute, she was gone. All that remained was gray, **smoldering** dust on the dungeon floor.

Razva sank to his knees beside the heap of ash. "Thank you, my young friends," he said. "I could not have done this without you."

Jack and Dylan were in shock. Finally, Jack stuttered, "Razva, did that just happen? Did we really kill a vampire?"

Razva looked up at the boys. "Yes, Jack," he said. "Vampires are real. And she's not the first one I've encountered."

"What do you mean?" asked Dylan.

"It was my **destiny** from birth to be a hunter of vampires," he said. "My father was a vampire hunter, as was my grandfather before him. My family members have hunted and destroyed these evil monsters for generations."

Jack and Dylan struggled to take this all in.

"When your sister wanted to get married here in Castle Prahova, I knew it could be dangerous," continued Razva. "But it was also a chance to find the creature that was imprisoned here many centuries ago."

Razva stood up. "Last night, after I was certain you were all safely locked in your rooms, I began my **quest** to search the castle and destroy the vampire."

Dylan looked at Jack. "I can't wait to tell Mom and Dad that Razva is a vampire hunter," he said breathlessly.

Razva placed his hands on Dylan's shoulders and looked into his eyes.

In a low, serious voice, he said, "You can tell no one, Dylan. My mission to hunt vampires must remain a secret."

"Can I trust you?" asked Razva. "Will you keep my secret?"

In stunned silence, the boys nodded their agreement.

"Excellent," said Razva giving the boys a friendly smile. "Now, we must get ready for the wedding. It is in a few hours."

As the boys followed Razva from the dungeon, they thought about his secret.

Jack snuck a look at his brother. Dylan looked back. Grins began to spread across the boys' faces. Without saying anything, each of the twins knew what the other was thinking:

How cool will it be to have a brother-in-law who's a vampire hunter!

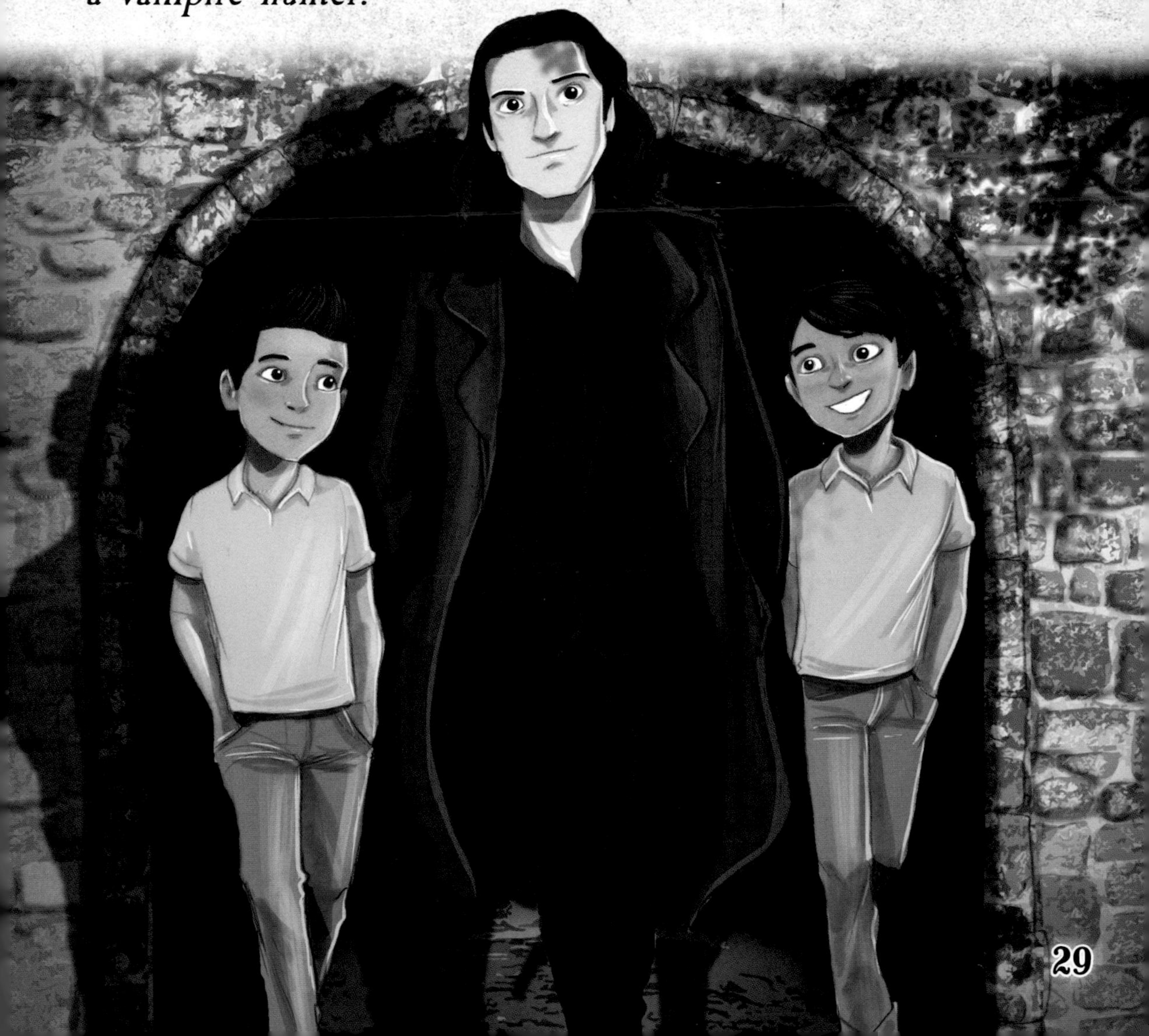

The Vampire's Lair

1. What do Jack and Dylan discover about Castle Prahova in the brochure?

2. Why are the twins suspicious of Razva? Use examples from the story to explain.

3. What has happened in this scene?

4. How do Razva and the boys kill the vampire?

5. How would you react if you found out vampire's were real?

GLOSSARY

ancient (AYN-shuhnt) belonging to a time long ago

corpse (KORPS) a dead body

courtyard (KORT-yard) an open area surrounded by walls

destiny (DESS-tuh-nee) something that has been decided beforehand

dungeon (DUN-juhn) a dark prison cell, usually underground

fiancé (fee-ahn-SAY) a man engaged to be married

gruesome (GROO-suhm) horrible and disgusting

iron maiden (EYE-urn MAY-din) a torture device large enough to hold a person, studded with sharp spikes on the inside

legend (LEJ-uhnd) a story from the past that is often not entirely true

medieval (meh-DEE-vuhl) from the time of the Middle Ages, around the 400s through the 1400s A.D.

puncture (PUNKT-shur) a hole or wound made by piercing with a sharp object

quest (KWEST) a journey to seek something out

rack (RAK) a torture device on which a person's body is stretched in order to cause great pain

smoldering (SMOHL-dur-ing) smoking and burning slowly with no flames

stake (STAYK) a thick, pointed piece of wood or metal

stench (STENCH) a terrible smell

suspicious (suh-SPISH-uhss) having questions or doubts

tapestries (TAP-uh-streez) cloth wall hangings with pictures woven into them

ABOUT THE AUTHOR

Dee Phillips develops and writes nonfiction books for young readers and fiction books—including historical fiction—for middle graders and young adults. She loves to read and write stories that have a twist or an unexpected, thought-provoking ending. Dee lives near the ocean on the southwest coast of England. A keen hiker, her biggest ambition is to one day walk the entire coast of Great Britain.

ABOUT THE ILLUSTRATOR

German-based illustrator Timo Grubing works on children's books, educational books, and magazines. When he's not working on projects for children, he enjoys drawing zombie comics. He lives and works in Bochum, Germany, in the heart of the Ruhr area, with his girlfriend, who is also an illustrator, and two cats, who do not have artistic dispositions.